SIMON & SCHUSTER BOOKS FOR YOUNG READERS
An imprint of Simon & Schuster Children's Publishing Division
1230 Avenue of the Americas, New York, New York 10020
Copyright © 2020 by Alex Willan
SIMON & SCHUSTER BOOKS FOR YOUNG READERS is a trademark of Simon & Schuster, Inc.
For information about special discounts for bulk purchases, please contact
Simon & Schuster Special Sales at 1-866-506-1949 or business@simonandschuster.com.
The Simon & Schuster Speakers Bureau can bring authors to your live event.
For more information or to book an event, contact the Simon & Schuster Speakers Bureau
at 1-866-248-3049 or visit our website at www.simonspeakers.com.
Book design by Chloë Foglia and Alex Willan • The text for this book was set in Rockwell.
The illustrations for this book were rendered digitally.
Manufactured in China • 0520 SCP • First Edition
2 4 6 8 10 9 7 5 3 1
Library of Congress Cataloging-in-Publication Data
Names: Willan, Alex, author, illustrator.
Title: Unicorns are the worst! / Alex Willan ; illustrated by Alex Willan.
Description: First edition. | New York : Simon & Schuster Books for Young Readers, [2020] | Audience: Ages 4 to 8 |
Audience: Grades K–3 |
Summary: A grumpy goblin hates having unicorns as neighbors, but when dragons threaten his home and the
unicorns come to the rescue, he has to admit that maybe unicorns are not so bad after all.
Identifiers: LCCN 2019033153 (print) | LCCN 2019033154 (eBook) |
ISBN 9781534453838 (hardcover) | ISBN 9781534453845 (eBook)
Subjects: CYAC: Goblins—Fiction. | Unicorns—Fiction. | Humorous stories.
Classification: LCC PZ7.1.W545 Un 2020 (print) | LCC PZ7.1.W545 (eBook) | DDC [E]—dc23
LC record available at https://lccn.loc.gov/2019033153
LC eBook record available at https://lccn.loc.gov/2019033154

For Erin, Camron, Emma, Leah & Reese

UNICORNS ARE THE WORST!

By ALEX WILLAN

Simon & Schuster Books for Young Readers NEW YORK LONDON TORONTO SYDNEY NEW DELHI

For hundreds of years I have gone about completing my important goblin business in peace.

From documenting spells,

to gathering ingredients for spells,

to alphabetizing the ingredients I've gathered for spells.
No distractions. No interruptions. Just me and my work.
But guess who decided to move into the meadow next door.

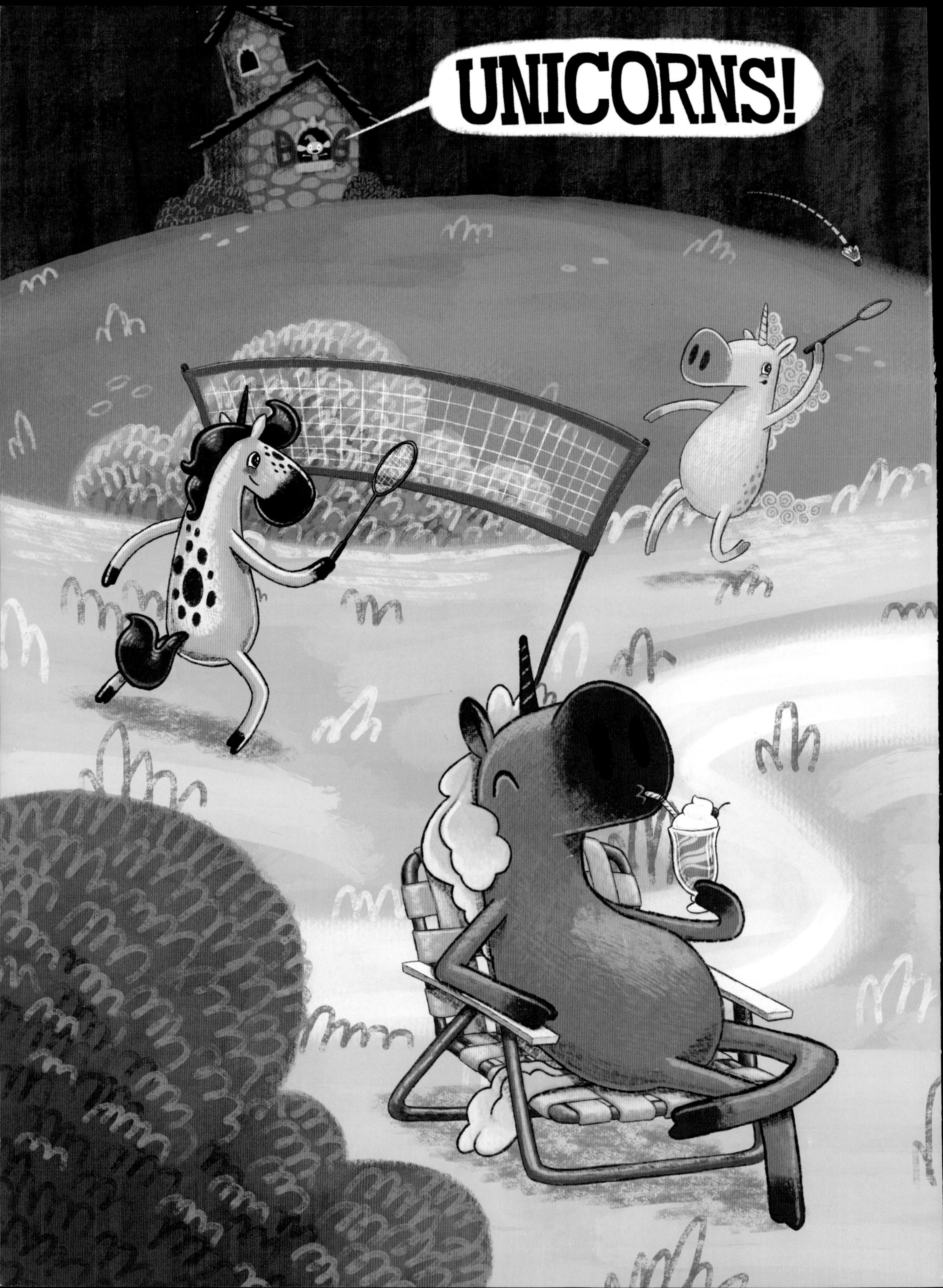
UNICORNS!

Now, I know what you are going to say. . . .

GOBLINS

I have studied the forgotten magic
that lies deep within the earth.

fig.1

fig.2

I know spells that can transform socks into slugs,

fig.3

fig.4 *

I can turn broccoli into ice cream,

* Still tastes like broccoli.

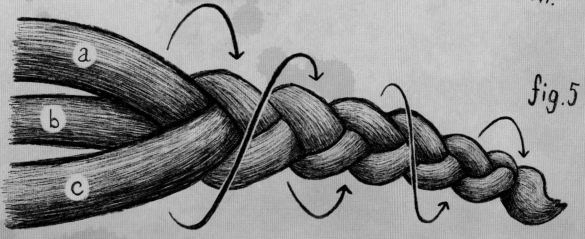

fig.5

and I have mastered the three-strand braid!

But despite all of this, does anyone ever ask to have a Goblin-themed birthday party?

Meanwhile, all unicorns do is frolic around all day on their dainty unicorn hooves.

Frolicking isn't even hard. Goblins can frolic—we just choose not to.

And the glitter . . .

SO.

MUCH.

GLITTER!

Do you realize how hard it is
to get glitter out of a smock?

They are constantly playing their instruments.
News flash, unicorns: Not everyone likes harp music!

And the tea parties!

SO. MANY.
TEA PARTIES!

It's not like they ever ask me to one of their tea parties. Not that I would have time for tea parties when there is all this important work to be done. It's not like this shrub is going to document itself.

Do I enjoy a good cup of tea? Perhaps the occasional crumpet? We'll never know, because someone around here has to take their work seriously.

You know what? I wouldn't go to one of their silly tea parties, even if they did ask me. You know why?

For instance, did you know that their glitter can put out dragon fire?
And that harp music can be quite disorienting.

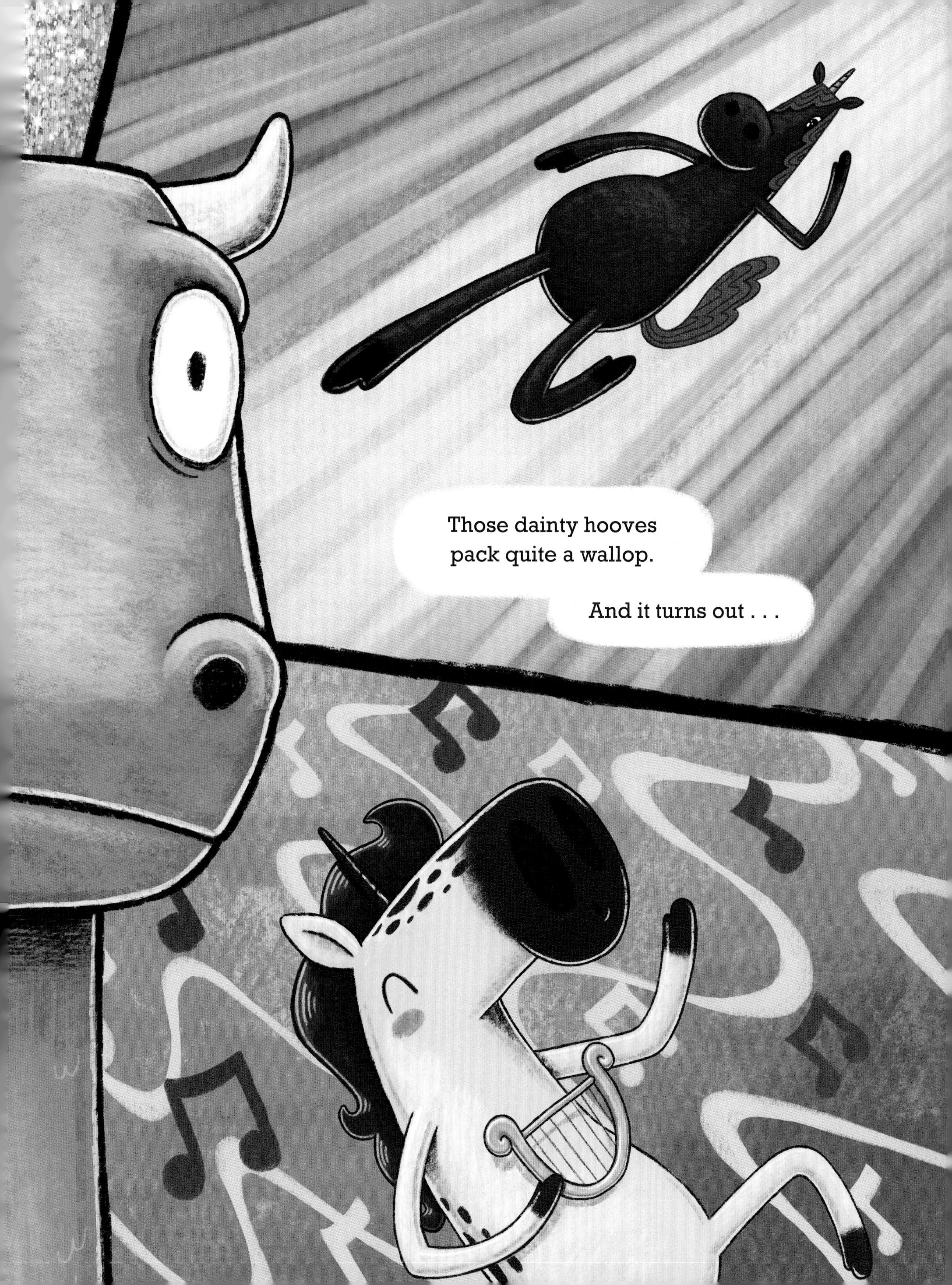
Those dainty hooves pack quite a wallop.
And it turns out . . .

All right, fine. As far as neighbors go, unicorns aren't *that* bad. But I think that we can all agree. . . .